ABOUT TH

Hûw Steer is an author and hi.   ᵤₘ London. He has
an MA in Ancient History, specialising in the study of
ancient science-fiction (yes, there is some!). His first novel,
The Blackbird and the Ghost, was a semi-finalist in the 5th Self-
Published Fantasy Blog-Off. He is currently having several
others rejected by agents and publishers.

This is his first book for children, with whom he spends
most of his time at The Toy Project in Archway.

Also by Hûw Steer:

Ad Luna

The Boiling Seas:

The Blackbird and the Ghost

Nightingale's Sword

Short Stories:

'A Discourse on the Prisoner's Cinema'
Phosphenes: UCL Publisher's Prize 2016

'A Conversation at the End of the World'
Light and Dark: UCL Publisher's Prize 2018

'The Vigil of Talos'
Making Monsters

'Blank Slates' *Shoreline of Infinity #19*

'The Only Cure' *Grimdark Magazine #25*

For more stories and updates from Hûw, visit
huwsteer.wordpress.com.

Contact him at huwsteerofficial@gmail.com.

THE FIRE WITHIN

The Adventures of Perce and Gideon

Book 1

Hûw Steer

First published with Kindle Direct Publishing in
2022

ISBN: 9798357284952

Cover art by Laura G. Wingrove
www.laurawingrove.com

Set in Garamond

For Ahmed, Aisha, Noa and all the other children at the
Toy Project.

1

Ten years ago

In the old man's hand, the fire burned.

Perce had only just turned two years old.
They barely knew what fire was – they barely
knew what *anything* was. They knew a handful
of words, could just about walk in a straight
line. Everything was confusing, bewildering,
new. Especially on a day like this: the spring
festival, when the whole village came out to
celebrate, filling the air with the smell of
cooking food, ribbons and banners of bright

colour, the sounds of music and laughter.

But when Perce saw the fire, they couldn't look away.

It was a perfect flame, yellow-orange and warm. It licked the air like a dragon's tongue. It filled the old man's palm, curling into the air above it. Small tendrils of fire wrapped themselves around the old man's fingers, but they didn't burn him. They didn't hurt him at all. This fire was the old man's friend.

Perce was only two. They didn't know how fire worked. They didn't know that the *oohs* and *aahs* of the watching crowd, of their watching parents (who were holding them up to watch the old man in the blue robes put on his show) weren't just about how pretty the fire looked. They were *oohs* and *aahs* of wonder, that the old man could hold the fire at all.

Perce didn't know what magic was yet. But they knew the fire was special. It entranced them. It called to them.

Maybe, Perce thought, *it will be my friend too.*

They reached out with their tiny hand, and stuck it straight into the flame.

Quite a few things happened at once then. Perce's mother screamed. Perce's father jerked backwards, taking Perce with him. The old man pulled the fire away at the same time, closing his hand and snuffing it out instantly. Other people started shouting too, calling for water, a doctor, a priest. Someone grabbed Perce's hand and stuck it in a beaker of water.

Perce wasn't sure why. The fire had been warm. But it hadn't hurt. It hadn't hurt at all. And when the doctor looked at Perce's hand, she called out that everything was fine: the child was unhurt. They must have not have touched the fire at all. Everyone, and everything, relaxed.

But Perce *had* touched the fire. They had felt it, hot on their skin – not painful but warm, friendly, happy. Nobody else seemed to realise this. For the next week, Perce's mother wouldn't leave so much as a candle within six feet of Perce.

Nobody else noticed, except the old man. When everyone calmed down, he raised his hands and conjured a shower of scintillating sparks that had everyone gasping in wonder once again.

But as he looked over the crowd, he looked at Perce. Perce looked back. And the old man nodded, as if to say: *Nice to meet you, friend of fire.*

The old man left the village the day after the fair. And over the next ten years, Perce learned and did so many things that they forgot almost everything about that day.

Except for the fire, and the way it had felt against their hand. It had been Perce's friend after all.

2

Ten years later

The good news was that all the chickens had escaped the flames. Perce wished that their parents would focus on that instead of the bad news, which was that Perce had accidentally set the coop on fire with the power of their mind.

Some friend you turned out to be, they thought at the embers of the fire. The hot coals smouldered happily, not sorry in the least.

They sat in the cottage's little kitchen, the smell of woodsmoke everywhere, and hung their head as their mother and father tried to combine amazement with annoyance, and the relocated chickens clucked their way around the room.

"Magic!" their father exclaimed. "What else could it be?" Both he and Perce's mother were lightly singed from trying to put the fire out. So was Perce, their face grey with ash. It had taken a lot of effort – as though the flames hadn't *wanted* to be extinguished.

"My mother always said my grandmother was a witch," said Perce's mother sagely.

"Your grandmother thought she was a frog," Perce's father pointed out. Their mother scowled.

"Well, where else can it have come from?" she asked, folding her strong arms across her apron. "I don't remember *your* old da casting any spells!"

"True," conceded Perce's father cheerfully. He was a big man with a big smile, and he turned that smile on Perce. "However it happened… it's amazing! Our own child, a magician!" He looked shocked, but proud. Perce smiled sheepishly.

Their mother was a big woman with a big scowl, and she turned *that* on Perce too. Perce squirmed, and tried to hide behind their shock of lightly singed hair.

"I didn't *mean* to do it," they said. "It just… happened."

It had been a long day. They'd gotten up at the crack of dawn to let the chickens out and feed them. Then they'd walked two miles to school in the next village, where they'd spent the day trying and failing to cram grammar and maths into their head. *Then* they'd walked all the way home, slipped and fallen in the mud, been laughed at by some other children, and when the time had come to get the uncooperative chickens back into their coop Perce had just *snapped*. They'd gotten angry.

They'd never set anything on fire by being angry *before*, in fairness, but their parents didn't think that was an excuse.

"I didn't *want* to set *anything* on fire," Perce protested. But they *had,* in their heart, they realised. They'd been angry, and it had just forced its way out of them, hot and burning and… well, fiery. Their father patted them on the head sympathetically.

"It wasn't your fault," he said. Perce's mother grumbled, but Perce could tell she agreed. She was just angry.

"The chickens," she said, "will have to sleep in your room until then." She shooed one of the birds out of her skirts.

"Mum," Perce said, gripping the edge of their chair in annoyance. The smell of burned wood seemed to grow stronger. Then their mother yelped in fear, and Perce realised that the chair was beginning to smoulder.

A few moments later, with Perce's red-hot hands firmly immersed in bowls of water, the conversation continued.

"Well, we can't have you running around burning down the village," their mother said sensibly. "You'll have to… learn. To control it. To do magic."

"How?" Perce asked. There was no witch or wizard in the village. As far as Perce knew there was no witch or wizard for a hundred miles. They'd heard stories from some of the other adults about travelling magicians or strange lights in the sky, but had never really believed them.

Perce's parents looked at one another strangely. Then, even more strangely, they looked at Perce's hand.

"The festival's in a few weeks," said Perce's father.

"Do you think…" Perce's mother trailed off.

"Every ten years," said Perce's father. "Like clockwork. Since my granddad's day at least. And I don't care what Wayland the smith says. It *was* real magic."

"I suppose we could ask," said their mother hesitantly. "But *just* ask." Perce's father nodded.

"Who are you talking about?" Perce asked.

"With a bit of luck," said Perce's mother, "you'll see, very soon. But for now… just… try and hold it in, please? A chicken-coop's expensive enough without you burning down the house too." She said it accusingly, and Perce fought back a growl of anger. *It wasn't my fault!* they wanted to shout. *I didn't mean to!* But whether she'd meant to or not… it had felt good. It had felt *right*.

Steam filled the air, and Perce realised that their hands had begun to *boil* the bowls of water. They spent half an hour with their hands in the ice-box to get them nice and cold before going to bed, just in case. But at least there was plenty of hot water to make tea.

3

A week later, Whetstone was still standing. The chicken-coop had been rebuilt, and, despite a few charred bits of furniture, Perce had mostly managed to keep the fire in check. They'd even helped their mother with the laundry – being able to boil water and dry damp clothes at a touch was quite useful, even if they did burn a hole in their father's best shirt.

Just in case, the family agreed that Perce should stay away from school, sending a note explaining that Perce was ill. It wasn't completely untrue. But though it was fun to be off for a few days, Perce quickly got bored. And when they got bored, they got frustrated.

And when they got frustrated…

Everyone, Perce included, was glad beyond words when the wizard rolled into town.

They saw the wagon coming from half a mile away. It was bright blue, and something huge and brass on its roof shone like the sun. When the two horses pulled it closer, Perce saw that it was a telescope, folded down to travel but still much longer than they were tall.

Almost everyone in Whetstone formed a crowd as the wagon drew up in the middle of the village square, the horses panting with effort. Perce fidgeted at their mother's side. For some reason they'd been made to wear their best clothes, their wild hair forced into something approaching neatness. They'd asked why everyone had come out, but their father had just told them to wait and see. *Well, now I can.* As the wagon rumbled to a halt, Perce read the letters picked out in flaking gold paint along one side:

Gideon the Effervescent and his Peripatetic

Planetarium; Alchemist, Diviner, Physician and Mage.

The back door of the wagon sprang open, and a man in blue robes hopped down. He was tall, spindly as a willow and with a grey beard so sharply pointed it could have cut wood. The rest of his head was bald and gleaming. He cut an imposing figure in his sweeping robes, surveying the crowd with an imperious stare.

And for some reason, Perce felt like they'd seen him before.

The old man's regal expression cracked into a broad grin.

"Good morning, Whetstone!" he boomed, and every adult in the crowd cheered. He beamed at the sound. "I see some of you remember me!" He snapped his fingers, and a stool was tossed out of the back of the wagon. The old man hopped up onto it. Perce stared, confused. All the other children in the crowd looked the same. But the adults were all smiling.

"For those of you who don't know me," the old man continued, "well, it has been a decade, after all. I'd have visited sooner, but –"

"There's so much world to see!" chanted all the adults in unison, before breaking into laughter. It was as though they'd heard the same speech many times before. The old man laughed with them.

"Indeed there is," he said. "But as it's been a while, let me reintroduce myself! I," he gestured at the sign on the wagon behind him, "am Gideon the Effervescent! Itinerant scholar, physician, alchemist… and magician." He clicked his fingers again, and the side of the wagon dropped open, revealing an interior crammed with wonders – and a thin man in a brown robe, who ducked hastily out of sight to reveal glittering vials, strange roots and herbs, and more books than Perce had ever seen in one place. There was a chorus of *oohs* and *aahs* from the crowd of villagers, Perce included. Gideon's grin got even wider.

"I bring cures for diseases," the old man

proclaimed, "spices from the far West, and knowledge of the stars themselves!" He grinned. "Oh, and this."

He clapped his hands over his head, and a shower of scintillating sparks burst into the air in a thousand colours. Perce's eyes widened in delight. The crowd applauded.

"Now, if I've timed this right," Gideon called, "I should have arrived in time for your spring festival?" There was a chorus of 'yeses'. "Wonderful!" the old man exclaimed. "In that case... I'll be in the usual place. Come and see me there!" He hurled another burst of sparks into the air, bowed, and hopped off his stool to a round of applause.

"A real wizard!" Perce said to their father, who nodded happily.

"Old Gideon's been coming here since *my* granddad was a boy," he explained. "He wanders all over the land, so we don't see him often. But every ten years, he comes back to Whetstone for the spring festival."

"And it's a good thing he does," said Perce's mother, whose face was not smiling, but grimly determined. "Come on. Let's go introduce you."

They pushed through the dispersing crowd to the wagon, where Gideon and the man in brown were checking their horses and preparing to move again.

"Excuse me," said Perce's mother. The wizard turned, looked at them, frowned, then smiled.

"Lilian and Jack Thatcher," he said warmly. "How could I forget?" He shook their hands warmly. "You did a grand job on my roof, Jack," he said, nodding at the wagon.

"No more leaks?" Perce's father asked.

"Oh, dozens," Gideon replied, "but none in the bit you fixed!" He chuckled. "Now, last time I saw you, you were holding a bouncing little…"

He looked down at Perce, and trailed off.

Their eyes met. And suddenly Perce knew exactly where they'd seen him before. They remembered the festival, the smells, the sounds. They remembered the old man with the handful of flames. They remembered touching them, and not being burned.

"Hello again," Perce said, looking up at the spindly old wizard. They weren't much more than half his height – they were small for their age, and the wizard was tall and thin as a beanpole. Gideon looked down, and smiled just slightly.

"Hello," he said. "You stuck your hand in my fire."

"Yep." Once, Perce might have been nervous. But now they could make fire with their mind. Talking to strangers didn't seem so scary anymore. Gideon looked at Perce with a critical eye.

"You're a lot bigger."

"You're a lot older," Perce countered. "And doesn't 'Effervescent' just mean 'bubbly'?"

"Perce!" their mother snapped, but Gideon was laughing.

"And you've gotten clever, too!" he chuckled. "You're right. Just don't tell anyone else."

"That's not all they've gotten," said Perce's father nervously, but Gideon waved him quiet.

"If I had to guess," he said, "I would say that – forgive me, child, what's your name?"

"Perce."

"That Perce recently started setting things on fire with her mind. Am I right?"

"Yes," said Perce's mother. "How did you know?"

"I knew ten years ago," said Gideon, "when she didn't get burned."

"They," said Perce. "Not 'she'." Gideon started, but then bowed slightly to Perce.

"They. My apologies."

"It's alright," Perce said. "I hadn't decided back then."

Gideon nodded.

"What did you burn?"

"The chicken-coop."

"How badly?"

"To the ground." Gideon grimaced.

"I'm afraid," he said to all three of them, "that magic can be a messy business."

"And an expensive one," muttered Perce's father.

"Quite," said Gideon with a thin smile.

"We were hoping you could… you could help," said Perce's mother carefully. "That you could… show Perce how. To control it."

Gideon frowned. "To do that," he said, "I must first see what 'it' is." He clapped his hands, turned to his wagon. "Clive!" he called.

"A little detour before lunch. Get us ready to go!" A muffled "Alright!" came from inside the wagon in reply.

"Come with me," said Gideon to Perce and their parents. "And we shall see exactly what Perce can do." He looked down at Perce. "Will you show me, Perce?"

Perce looked up at the strange old man. And though they didn't quite trust him yet, they could see that his bright eyes were filled with curiosity.

"Alright," they said. Because after all, they wanted to see what they could do too.

4

"It's all about focus," Gideon said, his eyes half-closed, one hand outstretched. He held a gnarled wand made of blackened, stained wood. "Power is no good if you cannot direct it to your will. Being a mage isn't just about great power – it is about knowing *when* great power is needed, and when it is not."

He twisted his hand slightly.

"For example. Here, a little magic will accomplish what a lot could not. I use the wand as my focus. I let my magic out, just a little. It flows *through* me…"

There was a sound of sizzling and popping, and Gideon opened his eyes in a flash.

"…and into this." He held the wand up in front of Perce. On the end was a sizzling sausage.

Perce had expected a magic lesson, not lunch. But by the time they'd ridden a mile outside Whetstone for safety's sake, their father's stomach had been rumbling. So they'd stopped the wagon in an empty, overgrown field, and to Perce's surprise Gideon had constructed and lit a campfire by hand.

"Magic is a wonderful thing," he'd said, "but some things have to be done the old-fashioned way." He had lit the fire with a clockwork lighter. Then, once it was nice and hot, he had begun to cook.

Clive the manservant put the sausage on a plate and handed it to Perce's mother. She looked at it dubiously.

"Try it," said Gideon eagerly. Reluctantly, Perce's mother sliced it open. The smell was delicious; beef and herbs; and inside it looked perfectly cooked. The outside was nowhere near as black and burned as something cooked on an open fire would be. *Magic,* Perce realised. *He cooked it from the* inside.

Perce's mother took a bite.

"Very nice," she said. "But a little overdone."

Gideon scowled.

"Damn. I thought I had it this time." He pulled a fat notebook from his robe and scribbled something – using his wand, Perce noticed, the tip blackening the page like charcoal. Clive chuckled.

"He's been at this for years," he said. "Convinced that magic is the only way to make the perfect barbeque." Clive had been introduced as Gideon's manservant, but Perce wasn't so sure. He and Gideon seemed more like an old married couple.

"I draw ever-closer by the meal," Gideon

proclaimed haughtily. "I've nailed sweetcorn."

"I'd love some sweetcorn," said Perce's father, holding out his own empty plate. Gideon smiled.

He *had* nailed sweetcorn. They all ate in near-silence, simply enjoying the food that the old wizard had made. Perce was oddly impressed. It wasn't anything like what they'd expected a wizard to do, but the results spoke for themselves.

When they'd finished, Gideon stood and brushed off his robes. He beckoned Perce over to join him a few yards away.

"Please watch," he said to their parents. "Though you may want to stand back." Perce's parents did so, standing nervously next to Clive. Perce looked at them, and their father gave them an encouraging nod. *Here goes,* they thought. They went over to Gideon.

"So," said the old wizard. "You've started setting things on fire."

"Yes."

"By accident?"

"Yes." It was still a little embarrassing even here. Gideon noticed, and smiled dangerously.

"Do you want to do it on purpose?"

There was a stand of dead trees in the middle of the meadow, the remnants of an orchard that had been hit by a storm decades ago and then cut down. A few stumps still jutted from the long grass. Gideon led the way until he and Perce were about twenty feet from the trees. Perce's parents and Clive hung back ten feet more. Gideon pointed at the leftmost tree.

"Burn it," he said.

Perce brushed their tangled fringe out of their eyes and looked at the tree. They could feel the fire beneath their skin, but they felt *calm* too, for the first time in days. They'd eaten well, and nobody had shouted at them in hours.

The one time I need to do it and I'm too relaxed to burn! they thought. It was annoying. It made them angry.

A patch of grass five feet to the left of the tree burst into flames. Perce heard their father yelp in surprise.

"Not a bad start," Gideon said, and he raised one hand and gestured, closing his hand abruptly. The fire extinguished itself instantly and completely, leaving nothing but charred grass and a wisp of smoke. Perce clenched their fists tightly, feeling the heat within their hands. Gideon made another gesture, slowly extending his arm and then splaying his fingers wide.

"Try that," he said, making the gesture again. "Use your hand as the focus. *See* the heat move, from your heart to your hand to the air."

Perce tried it. They thrust their hand forward, snapped their fingers open, and felt the rush of heat as it left their hand and went towards the tree. And *past* the tree, into the long grass behind it. Gideon made the hand-closing gesture again and put the fire out.

"Now try aiming," he said, smiling to take the sting out of the words. He performed the motion again. "Keep visualising the flame. Imagine a line, from your fingers to the tree."

"Why can't I see it?" Perce asked. Gideon frowned.

"What, the fire?"

"I thought fireballs were meant to be… balls," they said. "Or streams. Something you can see."

"They will be," Gideon explained. "Once you're using actual *fire*." He snapped his fingers, and on the end of his thumb a small flame burst into life. He dipped his thumb towards his open palm, and suddenly he was holding an entire handful of flames, crackling merrily but not burning him at all. It was exactly what he'd done ten years ago. Perce could hear their parents whispering as much to each other. They watched the fire hungrily.

"You," said Gideon, "are channelling *heat,* not fire proper. It has similar results, but there are several important distinctions. You're not ready for the true flame just yet."

Perce frowned. *I'm not, am I?*

They tried to set the leftmost tree on fire three more times, and on the last attempt they managed to hit the tree dead-centre, the dry, dead trunk bursting into flames. Gideon nodded approvingly. Perce's father clapped.

"Good. You're getting the connection." He clenched his fist, hard, and the fire went out. "Now," Gideon said, "try the centre one. Focus. Connect. And let the magic flow."

Perce looked at the tree in the centre. They could feel the heat surging in their veins. It *wanted,* badly. Not just to be out of them, but to… become. It was magic, it was heat, but it could be more. They remembered the fire in Gideon's hand, how they had touched it as a baby and felt nothing but warmth.

I was ready for fire then, they thought. *Why not now?*

Perce concentrated, and raised their hand, palm up. *Go on then,* they told their magic. *Become.*

Their palm smoked, then sparked, and then a bright ball of fire bloomed there, orange and yellow and beautiful. Perce laughed aloud, triumphant.

Then they felt pain, hot as the fire, and screamed when they realised their skin was burning.

5

This time, Gideon did not just wave his hand. As Perce screamed, he swore loudly, drew his wand, and said something fast and rhythmic that Perce didn't understand. He waved the wand, raised his hand, and water burst from his palm, a great jet of it, dousing Perce's hand in sudden, freezing cold. But the fire *did not go out*. It burned on Perce's palm, fighting against the cold water, still trying to scorch their skin. The magic was fighting to stay alive, trying to *keep being* what it had become.

Then Perce's mother was there – not screaming, not panicking, but completely focused. She had her cloak wrapped around

Perce's hand in seconds, smothering the fire.

"More water!" she snapped at Gideon, and the wizard shot more water from his hand, soaking the thick wool. But Perce could see the wet wool starting to smoulder even so.

"Lilian," said Gideon, his voice strained as he kept the water flowing, "when I say, take the cloak away."

"She's still burning!" Perce's mother snapped.

"Please *trust me,*" Gideon said earnestly. "Perce, when your mother removes the cloak, *close your hand,* and *focus.* This fire is yours. You control it. You *can* put it out." He tried a reassuring smile. It didn't work.

Perce felt their father's big hands on their shoulders. They couldn't see him, but they heard him say, "Lil, listen to him." Their mother paused, then nodded.

"One," said Gideon. He dropped his wand and raised his own free hand "One." Perce braced themself. "Two." They felt the fire surge stronger, and gritted their teeth.

"Three."

Perce's mother whipped the wet cloak away, and Gideon and Perce both snapped their hands shut.

For a horrible moment, the fire still burned, flames forcing their way between Perce's closed fingers. But then, finally, Perce felt the heat fade, and the fire was gone.

They opened their hand, and saw raw, red skin and a hundred blisters. Then it started to *really* hurt.

Perce said several words through their clenched teeth that they weren't supposed to know, including the one Gideon had used earlier. It hurt worse than anything they'd ever felt. But their mother was there, and their father, and they were wrapping the burn in the cool, damp cloak again, holding them gently.

"You're alright," their father was

murmuring. "You're alright, Perce."

"It *hurts*," Perce whimpered. It really, *really* did.

"I have salves," said Gideon, "in the wagon." He suddenly looked every one of his many years. "Please."

Perce's father picked them up as though they were a bag of feathers. He carried them gently back to the wagon, where Clive had already brought out several jars of ointments and salves. Perce's mother took them from him, examined them carefully, then nodded curtly.

"This will do," she said, and opened a jar. Whatever was inside smelled disgusting. But when she rubbed it into Perce's blistered skin, it started to hurt a little less.

"I couldn't stop it," Perce said softly. They felt tired, like they hadn't slept in a week.

"Which is why," Gideon said as he crouched down next to them, "I said you weren't ready." He grimaced. "Fire is hungry, Perce. Once it starts to burn, it is hard to stop."

"But it didn't hurt me before," Perce protested. "When I was little." They'd been so sure that the fire wouldn't hurt – they were its *friend*.

Weren't they?

"Yes," said Perce's mother – and the anger in her voice was hotter than any fire. "Why *did* it hurt this time?"

"When you touched *my* flames," Gideon said wearily, "it was different. To you, it was just fire. Your magic could keep you safe from that. But this was *your* fire. Your magic. And if you are not careful, if you don't know how…"

"It can hurt you," finished Perce's mother, glaring at Gideon.

"I did say Perce wasn't ready," the wizard said.

"But not *why*," Perce's mother replied

angrily. "You should have said *why*."

"Let's have this argument *later*," said Perce's father, raising his hands to stop any further snapping. "Perce, let's get you home, alright?" Perce nodded wearily. Home sounded good. Their bed was at home. It was warm, and… soft… and…

6

Perce woke up in their own bed, to the sound of voices below.

Perce sat up, and immediately fell back down when they put pressure on their burned hand. Trying again, they made it upright. There was a cup of water next to the bed and they drank it greedily, before looking nervously at their hand. It was neatly bandaged, with some sort of ointment staining the strips of cloth green from beneath. Perce recognised their mother's work. She wasn't *officially* the village doctor, but she might as well have been.

The bandages looked just like the ones the

blacksmith's boy had worn for two months when he'd pulled the wrong metal bar from the forge-fire without gloves. Thanks to Perce's mother, there had barely been a scar. Perce hoped that they'd be as lucky. The hand throbbed, but they could still move their fingers stiffly.

Their room was small – the whole house was small. The kitchen took up most of the ground floor, and the space under the shingled roof was just enough for a big bedroom – for their parents – and the tiny space at the end where Perce slept. When it rained, Perce could hear every drop drumming on the roof – but it had never leaked. Their father was very good at his job. And they liked the noise anyway. It was soothing.

There was a bed, and a chest for their clothes, and a shuttered window that overlooked the street. Their father had built a clever little shelf over the headboard where Perce kept interesting things: a battered book of stories, a shiny rock, a piece of wood that looked like a witch's hand. It was tiny, it was cramped. But it was home.

And because the house was so small, it was impossible *not* to hear other people's conversations. So Perce leaned back on their pillows and listened to what their parents were talking about below.

"…dangerous," came their mother's voice. "I'm not putting them in harm's way."

"Love, everything's dangerous eventually," pointed out their father. "Farming, smithing, hunting. Perce could get hurt in any of those jobs. It's just not so… spectacular."

"It is a difficult thing to come to terms with," came another, melodious voice, and Perce took a moment to realise that it was Gideon. "But please understand, Lilian, that my first priority is to show Perce how to *not* hurt themselves. The only way to do that is to teach them."

"Teach them to throw fire," said Perce's mother. "Teach them to burn things, to destroy."

"And to create," Gideon said, so softly that Perce could barely hear him. "Magic can do that, too, with practice." There was a pause. Perce heard their father gasp in appreciation of whatever Gideon was doing.

"Cheap tricks," said Perce's mother, "won't work, 'Master' Gideon.

"No," said Gideon. "Forgive me. But apart from keeping them safe, training could make Perce…" He trailed off, searching for the right words. "I have not taught an apprentice," he said finally, "in many years. I am out of practice. But I *have* taken students before, and I have lived a very long time. And I tell you now that Perce is the most naturally gifted magician I have ever seen."

Perce felt a little glow of pride at that.

"They set themselves on fire," said their mother, and the glow went out.

"It took me six months before I could so much as conjure a candle-flame," said Gideon. "And Perce is *strong*. I have been a magician for longer than anyone in this village has been alive, and I couldn't put Perce's fire out."

"I noticed," said Perce's mother icily.

"Come on, Lil," said Perce's father. "The man's saying Perce has talent. We can't let them waste that. Especially if they might get hurt." His voice turned to iron. "Because they'd better not get hurt again."

"You know I cannot promise that," Gideon sighed. "But they are far more likely to be hurt without proper training than with it. I *can* promise that I will give them that training."

"But how bad could it be?" Perce's mother asked. "How bad *could* it have been, if we weren't there?"

Perce looked at their bandages, and frowned. They'd been so caught up in the joy of it all… how badly *could* magic go wrong?

Was it worth the risk?

They thought of the painful burns, how scary it had been to lose control. But then

Perce thought of the beauty of the flames. The flames they'd made. The things *they* would be able to do.

They were out of bed and on the stairs before their mother could speak again, almost tumbling down in their haste to interrupt. They shoved through the kitchen door, to find all the adults looking up at them in surprise and relief. Gideon and Perce's parents were sitting at the table, all holding mugs. Clive had the teapot in his hands.

"I want to learn," Perce said quickly, before anyone could interrupt. "I *have* to learn. Learn more, be better." They raised their bandaged hand, the words tumbling out of their mouth in no particular order. "I'll be careful. I'll be safe. But I have to learn." They looked at their mother and father. "Please."

Their father smiled a little. Their mother couldn't take their eyes off the bandages. But Clive cleared his throat.

"If I may?" He put down the teapot. "I

have spent much of my life," Clive said, "patching this one back together." He squeezed Gideon's shoulder, and Gideon patted his hand fondly. "It was a bad burn," Clive continued, walking over to Perce. "But having magic has other benefits." He glanced at Perce's mother questioningly. She nodded. Clive took Perce's hand, and carefully unwound the bandages. Perce braced themself… but there were no blisters anymore. The skin was still red, still painful – but to their amazement, the burn was already halfway healed.

"Magic," said Gideon, a little proudly. "It can burn, but it can grow too."

"Well that's handy," said Perce's mother weakly. Perce flexed their stiff fingers and marvelled. Their parents looked at one another meaningfully. Gideon and Clive sat back quietly.

"Perce," said their father, "do you want to do this?"

"More than anything," Perce replied. Their parents exchanged another glance, then nodded.

"Then I suppose you better had," said their mother with a reluctant smile.

7

Perce looked at the word. It looked back at them, stubborn and unreadable. They tried to sound it out, but it just turned into a noise like a dying frog. They scowled, and shoved the book away across the kitchen table.

"Perce," warned Gideon. Perce looked at the book, whose pages were giving off little wisps of smoke. They took a deep breath, and repeated their mantra. It was the first thing Gideon had taught them.

I am the flame and the water. I am slave to neither. They repeated it quietly three times – it was much the same as counting slowly to ten.

When they had finished, they were still annoyed, but no longer angry.

On the other side of the table, their mother put down the large jug of water she'd been about to throw, and went back to her knitting. But her eyes never left Perce and Gideon.

The arrangement that Perce's parents and Gideon had hammered out was as follows: for four days a week, Gideon would teach Perce from morning until afternoon. The lessons would either be in Gideon's wagon or at Perce's house, depending on Perce's parents' schedule. At least one of them, Perce's mother had insisted, would be present at all times, just in case – and with a bag of medicines close by. On the fifth day, Perce would go to the school in the next village as normal. *"Learning magic is all well and good,"* Perce's father had said, *"but you're still twelve. You've got to know your numbers and all that too."*

Perce had hesitantly asked about just travelling with Gideon instead, but everyone had shaken their heads.

"Maybe one day," their father had allowed. *"But not yet."* Gideon had nodded agreement.

"You have much to learn," he had said, *"before you leave your home. Magic or not."* Perce's mother had nodded approvingly at that. *"In a few years,"* Gideon had continued, *"there are places we would do well to visit, to further your education. The Convocation in the High City, the Fountainhead, things like that."* Perce had perked up at that. They had heard those names before, in old stories.

"But not yet,*"* Perce's mother had repeated firmly. *"When you're older, and you've learned a lot more."* And that, apparently, was that.

Gideon cleared his throat, and Perce's attention jolted back to the present.

"Repeat after me," said the old wizard. *Incendiary."*

"Incendiary."

"Now read it off the page." He pushed the book towards them again. Perce looked at the stubborn word, and mouthed it over and over, matching the sounds to the letters. Gradually, it made sense.

"Now the whole sentence," Gideon said, seeing that they had it. Perce cleared their throat.

"Proper control of… *incendiary* spells and magics is essential, to avoid their… *combustive* side-effects and prevent injury, to the caster and to those around them." It was a mouthful, but Perce at least understood it. "I have to be careful with fire because I could burn down the village."

"Essentially."

"I know that already."

"I know you do," Gideon explained. "But you have to learn your theory. Which means, I'm afraid, reading some of these." He patted the enormous pile of books Clive had brought from the wagon. They were huge, leatherbound, dusty, and very, *very* wordy.

"I can *read*," Perce said stubbornly. They just didn't *want* to.

"Then read this," Gideon said, pointing to a sentence further down the page. Perce looked at it. The writing was cramped, the words were long, and Perce was certain that half of them were made-up. They glowered up at Gideon, who chuckled.

"I'm afraid magicians suffer terribly from having enormous egos. We're all convinced that we're fabulous writers, and that nobody will ever write a better book of magic than we will." He waved an arm at the pile of books. "Hence this."

It was just a few books from what was, according to Clive, only a fraction of Gideon's library – as much as he could carry in the wagon without the axles breaking. Clive had told Perce that his master had apartments in the High City with enough books to fill Perce's house from floor to ceiling. But there were still more books in the wagon than Perce had ever seen, three or four times what even Father

Tully, the village priest, had. There were books on herbs, on medicine, on mathematics, and quite a few interesting-looking novels. But mostly, there were books on magic. *Lots* of books on magic. Like the ones in front of them now.

"Will I have to read all of them?" Perce asked warily. Gideon laughed aloud.

"Even *I've* not read all of them," he confessed. "Not cover-to-cover. Each one has useful sections and good ideas. But none of them are the definitive 'best book'."

Perce noticed a title halfway up the stack. *Thaumaturgy and its Effects on the Natural World.* By Gideon of Tulsa, Called The Effervescent. Gideon caught them looking.

"Even that one," he sighed, "despite my best efforts. The point is, Perce, that there is much even we old wizards do not know about magic. We are all of us still learning. And if you are to learn from these books, and from me, then you will have to learn to read them." He smiled. "Who knows? Perhaps some day there will be a book by Perce of Whetstone on my shelf."

It wasn't a thought that had ever crossed Perce's mind before. Still, they thought, as they bent over the next page, it was a nice image.

8

On the fourth day, the bandages came off Perce's hand. The skin was still a bit pink, but it didn't hurt a bit. That meant it was time to start doing *real* magic again.

Gideon had parked his wagon on the outskirts of Whetstone, where it could back onto a fallow field. It was the perfect place to practice: there was lots of space, and – once some sheep had been moved – it was far enough away from anything important that might burn down.

This time, they had an audience. In the evenings, after Perce had finished their lessons,

the villagers of Whetstone had started coming
to Gideon for his other services: medicines,
divination, and all sorts of strange words. A
few of them were already queuing outside the
wagon, chatting to Perce's father, who was
leaning on the fence, waiting. When Perce
followed Gideon into the field, they could hear
their father proudly pointing out that yes, that
was his child, the apprentice wizard. Gideon
laughed when he saw the spectators.

"A lesson in life," he said to Perce.
"Nobody will ever turn down a free show."

Clive straightened up from a folding table
and nodded amiably to Perce. Clive didn't say
much and often kept to himself, but when he
did make a dry joke it sent Gideon into
hysterics. They would needle one another
gently, and were seldom seen apart for long.
They were obviously at least fast friends, and
had been for a long time.

"All ready," Clive said, gesturing to his
efforts. There were three large glass jars on the
table, filled with water. In each one there

floated an egg.

"Thank you, Clive," Gideon said. "See to the rest of lunch, if you wouldn't mind." Clive nodded, and walked back to the wagon.

"Now," Gideon said to Perce, "what do you think we're going to do here?"

Perce looked at the eggs and the water, and thought about all the reading they'd been doing. It was a test of what they could do. That meant heat. Heat, water, and eggs. They thought for a moment.

"The rest of lunch", Gideon had said.

"You want me to cook them," Perce said. Gideon beamed.

"Precisely. To be precise, I want you to cook them *differently.* I like my eggs hard-boiled. Clive likes them runny. You, I believe, are somewhere in-between." Perce frowned. Gideon smirked. "I asked your mother."

"Is there one for me?" called Perce's father from the fence. Some of the villagers chuckled.

"You were supposed to pack your own lunch, Jack," Gideon called back, to more laughter. He turned back and pointed at the eggs.

"Start with hard-boiling," he said. "I'll help you on this one." He produced an ornate brass disc from his robe, flipped open its lid, and revealed a clock with far too many hands. "Heat the water to boiling, and then hold it there. This is about timing and precision." He raised the watch. "Start… *now.*"

Perce concentrated, and reached out with their mind. They felt the water sitting there, a great cold mass. They touched it, focused on it, and let their magic flow. When they opened their eyes, the water was already bubbling.

Gideon glanced at his watch.

"And… stop." Perce let go of the magic. Gideon waved his wand, and the egg floated out of the bubbling water, into a silver egg-cup held by Clive, who had appeared at just the right time. He also had a plate of toast, and two more cups. Gideon took the cup and sliced the top off the egg. It was nicely hardboiled.

"Good," he said. "Now try Clive's. Just as hot, but not as long."

Perce concentrated. This time they heated the water more slowly, letting just a trickle of their magic out. It was hard to keep it so controlled. They waited, counting in their head, and then said, "Now." Gideon raised the second egg, and Clive caught it in his cup. He cut the top off, revealing gooey golden yolk.

"A little longer than normal," he said, "but perfectly nice. Thank you, Perce." Perce grinned.

"Now the tricky one," Gideon said through a mouthful of egg and toast. "The middle. Boil it how you like it, Perce."

Perce was feeling a little tired now. But they concentrated, and brought the water to a boil with one hand, taking their eggcup and some toast from Clive with the other. It was easier when they pointed at the water – they sort of understood what Gideon had said about 'focuses'. They counted in their head again. They'd boiled plenty of eggs before. Just not like this.

When they thought it had been long enough, Perce said nothing. Instead, they concentrated on the water. It felt hot to their mind now, full of energy, or magic. Out of curiosity, they reached out, and *pulled*. The bubbles in the water died away. Perce reached out and plucked the egg from the water before Gideon could stop them. The egg was hot – but the water was cold. Gideon poked it with a disbelieving finger. Perce put the egg into its cup, and held up their plate of toast. It had been light brown before. Now it was almost black.

"You asked Mum about the egg," they said, "but not the toast. I like it well-done."

When they sliced open the egg, it was cooked to perfection. Behind the fence, Perce's father cheered.

"Now that," Gideon said, watching Perce as they crunched into a slice of toast, "was quite impressive." He waited until Perce swallowed. "Tell me how you did it."

"It was easy," said Perce. "The heat was already there. I just moved it somewhere else." From the water into the bread, to be precise.

Gideon raised an eyebrow.

"'Easy,'" he echoed. "You just skipped another month of lessons. And it was *easy*." Perce grinned, and Gideon did too. "You'll be on barbeque in no time," he said.

9

Perce stayed in the shadows and watched.

It was Saturday, and so their first week of lessons was over. Gideon was very pleased with their progress, and so were their parents. Perce hadn't set anything on fire by accident in days. By using their magic so much they'd stopped it from building up and overflowing. The calming exercises Gideon had taught them helped too. Perce felt tired – mentally and physically – but they felt good. For the first time in a long time it felt like they were doing something worthwhile.

Or it had, until yesterday, when they'd

gone back to their 'normal' school, and everything had been… different. And now it was Saturday, and all the other kids had come to town.

Whetstone was one of the bigger villages in the region. Perce's old school might have been in the next village over, but on the weekends most of the local children would all come to Whetstone to hang out. There was a market every other week, lots of good fields and trees for games – and now there was a wizard. And a wizard's apprentice.

A wizard's apprentice who felt… left out.

All the other kids were crowded around Gideon's wagon, standing on each other's shoulders to try and get a peek inside. Perce knew that Gideon wasn't there – he and Clive had gone out that morning to give the horses a bit of exercise. But something made Perce hang back, standing in the shadows of the house next door.

Perce had walked back into the classroom

and sat down just like normal. The lessons had been just the same as ever – even though Perce had missed a few days they'd caught up quickly. (After struggling though Gideon's ancient magic books, school comprehension was easy.)

But all day, everyone had been looking at Perce. Like they'd been waiting for them to do something. To do *magic*.

And Perce hated it.

They hadn't told anyone where they'd been, even though everyone *knew* already. It was hard to keep secrets in a little town like Whetstone. Perce had overheard people talking about them all day. But Perce kept quiet. Because they knew that if they mentioned it, they'd have to *show* everyone… and even after a week's learning it wasn't like they could *do* anything impressive yet. They could boil water, maybe set a tree on fire – but they'd promised their parents not to burn anything bigger than their fist without permission. It wasn't like they could lift rocks with their mind. *Yet.*

Perce had spent all day sat with their friends, in the same room, learning the same things as ever. But all day, they'd felt *different*. Out of place.

Was this what it was going to be like forever now? The 'different' one, the special case? Perce had already heard the other kids muttering jealously about how Perce was getting 'special lessons' from the wizard.

They wanted to do magic. They wanted to *be* special. But at the same time, Perce wanted to just be the same as always.

The sound of hooves on cobbles filled the air, and the kids yelled in delight as Gideon rode down the street, robes and beard flapping in the wind. They crowded around the two horses as Gideon tried to make his way back to the wagon, laughing at their antics.

Perce stayed in the shadows and watched. It was easier.

10

"Those children," Gideon said, shaking his head. He took a cup of tea from Clive and added milk. "Always the same. They'll tear your doors down until you at least show them some dancing lights." Perce shrugged. They had been good dancing lights, many-coloured and entrancing. When the children had demanded *more* magic, Gideon had provided it by plucking a football from one boy's hands and launching it across Whetstone with a wave of his wand. Everyone had run after it. Everyone except Perce, who had taken the chance to dart over the road and into Gideon's wagon.

Perce shrank down in their seat as someone walked past, waving through the wagon's open side. Gideon waved back cheerily. It didn't seem to bother him that, most of the time, his whole life was on display to every passer-by.

"I assume," Gideon said, motioning for Clive to pour another cup of tea for Perce, "that at least some of them are your friends." Perce shrugged.

"Sure."

"But you're not with them."

"Bit tired," Perce muttered.

"Or are you avoiding them?" Gideon asked. Clive passed Perce the mug of tea. Perce poured in a bit of milk, and shrugged.

"Don't feel like playing." The tea was a little too hot, and without thinking Perce pulled some of the heat into themselves. It simmered there with the rest of their magic.

"I'm sure you don't," Gideon said. "But I

think you should. At least go and sit with them." He gestured around the wagon. "They'll forget about me by the afternoon, at least for a while. I've dealt with children before."

"They'll want to see you set something on fire," Perce warned, and Gideon chuckled.

"I know. Which is why I won't, until the very day I leave town. *Then* they'll be ecstatic when I come back. Always leave your audience wanting more."

"Is that more wizard advice?"

"Acting advice, dear child." Gideon laughed at Perce's face. "Who better to play the wise old man than a wise old man? I sang with Mirren once, I'll have you know." Perce didn't know who that was, but Gideon hadn't finished. He put his teacup down.

"It is hard being different," he said. "I know. I may not look it –" he stroked his long beard meaningfully "– but I was young once too. I discovered my power around your age.

My life changed that day. I had to leave my school, my family."

"Why?" It was the first Perce had heard about how Gideon had become a wizard.

"Things were different back then," Gideon explained. "If you had magic, you went to the Academy, or you hid. Most people still go there even now."

"The Academy?"

"A university. It teaches all things, but magic especially. Mages run it. When I was a boy, they ran it with an iron grip." He grimaced. "I didn't have a choice. Though in fairness nobody in my village wanted me around either." He saw Perce staring and winked. "You burned down a chicken-coop," he said. "I burned down an inn."

Perce had to admit that they would probably have kicked Gideon out too.

"So I went off to the High City and I trained there," Gideon continued. "It was very strange, at first. On the one hand there were plenty of other children there. On the other, they were all either much older or younger than me. And they knew what they were doing. Even the young ones seemed to be better wizards than I was already." The old man looked sadly out of the wagon's window. "I was very lonely for a while."

He shook himself, and grinned.

"Then I realised that none of it mattered. The age difference, the skill difference. We were all children, all away from home and learning to be something extraordinary. We were *all* lonely. And so in time none of us were."

"But I'm the only one," Perce said. "The only one here." They drank a mouthful of tea to hide the sudden sadness, but Gideon shook his head.

"The only one learning magic? True, I'll grant you. But not the only one who feels like this." He looked out of the window. "I can hear them coming back already. They're quick." He looked back at Perce. "You are all children, magic or not. You are all young, all uncertain what the future holds. You are all lonely in your own ways.

"So go out there and be lonely together."

Perce thought about it.

"If we're together," they said, "then we can't be lonely. We're not alone." Gideon rolled his eyes.

"Stubborn child," he said. "You know what I mean."

"I do," Perce admitted, and finished their tea. "Alright. I'll go."

They paused at the wagon door.

"Do you still get lonely?" they asked. "Now?"

Gideon stroked his beard.

"For the most part? No. I have Clive, and I have my books." He smiled sadly. "But sometimes, yes. Even now. But it gets easier."

Perce nodded. That would do. They hopped down from the wagon, and went to play.

11

Perce had to run to catch up, but they reached the village square just behind the other children. They ran up and tapped the nearest on the shoulder.

"Hey."

"Hey!" It was Ben Fisher, the imaginatively-surnamed fisherman's son, who beamed with surprise. "Where have you been?"

"Chores," Perce explained. The lie passed muster.

"Well we're gonna play in the meadow,"

Ben said, gesturing over his shoulder. The village square was just beginning to fill with people, impromptu market stalls springing up left and right. The inn had opened its doors and set chairs and tables out in the square, and the smell of food was everywhere. At the edge of the square were a handful of other children, waiting for Ben to come back.

"Lunch first?" Perce asked, and Ben's stomach rumbled on cue.

"Yeah, maybe," he admitted. He shouted for the other kids to join them, and together they all went in search of food. Through a mixture of begging and bartering they furnished themselves with bread, cheese and a little fruit, and triumphantly strode off towards the designated meadow.

The grass was kept short by a small herd of sheep, who trotted away to the far corner of the field as soon as the children came into view. They knew what was about to happen, and didn't like footballs to the face any more than Perce. A set of crude wooden posts had been built at either end of a big rectangle marked in whitewash, covering about half the field. Perce was proud of the slightly wonky pitch. The children had made it themselves, borrowing the paint from Perce's father and building the posts out of scrap wood filched from the carpenter's yard. It wasn't exactly professional, but it was *theirs*.

They sat down in the middle of the field and ate and chatted. Perce fended off most of the questions about Gideon, about the magic. They shot a glance to Ben and their friend Annie, the mason's daughter, though – the sort of glance that meant *tell you later* – and the two of them nodded back. Conversation turned to the last week of school, which, as Perce hadn't been there, took the spotlight off them, and they sat back and just listened.

Eventually, someone picked up the football, and it was time to play. There was the usual round of arguments over who was on what team, and how to tell the teams apart – eventually they all decided on hat versus bare heads – and then someone kicked off. Perce had ended up in goal for the bare heads, which was good. They'd been working their brain hard for the last few weeks, but not their body. They didn't feel like running hard.

There *were* rules to their version of football, but they weren't exactly well enforced. Chaos erupted around the ball immediately, before Ben Fisher broke free from the tangle of limbs and sprinted… towards Perce, his cloth cap threatening to blow off his head. Perce tensed, leapt towards the ball as it flew… and missed by a finger, letting it through the goal. There were groans and cheers, but Ben was probably the best at football out of all of them. Nobody minded giving a goal to him. Perce punted the ball back to the middle of the field and readied themself again.

They saved the next goal, and then their team scored, the blacksmith's apprentice delivering a thunderous kick from halfway down the pitch that took the hats' goalie completely by surprise. Perce grinned happily. The action was in the other half of the pitch, so Annie, one of the defenders, wandered over to chat.

"Where *were* you, Perce?" she asked.

"Special lessons," Perce said. They both kept their eyes on the ball as they talked.

"With the wizard?" Annie said.

"…yeah," admitted Perce. "He's teaching me."

"My dads said they were watching the other day," Annie said. "You were boiling water or something?"

"I'm only just learning," Perce grumbled.

"It's still cool," said Annie earnestly. Perce glanced at her and smiled.

"Yeah," they said. "It is." And then there was no more time to talk because Ben was charging back down the pitch again, the ball at his feet. Annie ran out to tackle him, slowed him for a few seconds, but then was sidestepped and left behind. Then the ball was once again flying at Perce.

Perce jumped for it, but they could tell they were going to be well short. They could feel the air moving in front of the ball, being pushed out of the way by its mass. They stretched, arms straining as they jumped… and stretched their mind too.

Perce's hands missed the ball by a good foot. But it still bounced away as though they'd slapped it as hard as they could.

The ball flew back towards the midfield, and both teams descended on it, shouting and laughing. Except for Ben, and Annie, who both stared at Perce. They'd been the only ones close enough. *They'd* seen what Perce had done.

Perce smiled sheepishly.

"Magic," they mouthed.

12

The game was over. The hats had won, as Perce had felt that using magic to save every goal was probably cheating – and wasn't quite sure how they'd done it in any case. It was also getting late; the sun was low in the sky and everyone had to be home for dinner. So the children went their separate ways, some walking off down the roads to neighbouring villages, some heading into Whetstone. Perce, Annie and Ben hung back and walked together, enjoying the sunset and the gentle breeze.

"So," Ben said when there was nobody else around. "When were you going to *show us?*"

"Today," Perce said. It was only half a lie. "I've been busy."

"Too busy for school?" Ben asked.

"They've got *magic school* now," Annie said gleefully. Perce rolled their eyes.

"It's still school," they said. "Still lots of reading and numbers and stuff." Many more numbers and formulas than Perce had been expecting, in fact, for magic.

"But also magic!" Ben whooped. He jumped in the air and slapped a hanging branch in excitement. "What can you do? Do you have a wand?"

"Not much and not yet!" Perce laughed. "It's slow going. Gideon says I have to learn the basics properly before I start doing spells and things."

"You can do fire," Annie pointed out. Ben frowned. "Their chicken coop burned down, remember?" Annie said, jabbing him gently in the ribs. Ben *ohed* in realisation.

"That was you?"

"Didn't mean to," Perce said, still somewhat ashamed of that. Now that they (mostly) had control of their inner fire, just thinking of that loss of control was embarrassing.

"Still cool," Ben said evenly. "Can you set other stuff on fire?"

"If I try. But I'm not allowed," Perce said quickly before Ben could make his next, obvious request. "Not big stuff."

Annie bent down and picked up a stick.

"This isn't big." Perce thought for a moment. There was no-one around, and it *was* only a stick…

They took the stick, and Annie and Ben clustered around them. Perce made them stand a *bit* further back, just in case. Then they concentrated. After the football game – and their impromptu magic of earlier – they were tired, but the more magic they did, the more their stamina improved. They reached within, and coaxed a little of their power to the surface. *Heat,* Perce thought. *Not flame.* But heat did the same job. The end of the dry stick smouldered, then lit with a small, wavering flame. It wasn't much. But Ben and Annie were transfixed.

"Woah," Ben said.

"Yeah," Annie agreed. "Wow."

Perce grinned, and then pulled the heat back out of the stick, feeling the little rush of energy as the magic returned. The flame went out, leaving just a little smoke. Annie took it back, eyes wide, holding it like a holy relic.

"I can't do much yet," Perce said, feeling awkward. "But I'm learning."

"Perce," said Annie, very seriously, "you're doing *magic.* Anything is incredible."

They started walking again, Perce blushing a little at their friends' silent attention.

"So you're gonna be a wizard, then?" Ben

asked.

"I guess."

"They never told us we could do *that* at school," he grumbled.

"You'd be a rubbish wizard, Ben," said Annie.

"Yeah I would," Ben admitted. "I'd set myself on fire trying to make water."

They laughed their way back into town.

13

Three weeks passed.

Perce's control over their powers grew better every day. Now they could boil water from six feet away, if they tried hard enough – but also use heat gently, to dry clothes or hair, which had pleased Perce's mother no end. They were still learning lots of theory, but it was slowly becoming less and less boring the more Perce understood. And at 'ordinary' school, with Ben and Annie and the others, things were just like they'd always been.

Gideon had settled comfortably into life in Whetstone, as the villagers got over the novelty of having a wizard around… and were suddenly too busy to pay much attention at all. The village spring fair was next week, and bunting was already being dragged up as the first few wandering traders rolled into town. Stalls and stages were being assembled, vegetables gathered, kegs of ale dragged out of cellars. Perce was excited. *Everyone* was always excited for the festival. But this year there was a *wizard*. The children at school, even the ones from other villages, could talk of nothing else.

Then one morning Perce's mother came into their room with a note.

"No rush," she said, making Perce pause getting ready. They were meant to be at the wagon today, with their mother, but they were still only half-dressed. "Gideon sent a message." She handed Perce the note, and Perce unfolded it.

Perce. Please come to the wagon at sundown today. I have something special planned for today's lesson. I suggest both your parents attend — they may find it interesting.

Gideon

"I don't know what he's up to," their mother said, "but your father saw him and Clive doing something to the wagon on his way back from the butcher." She still didn't quite trust Gideon, even after watching him teach Perce for a month already. Sometimes Perce caught her looking at their healed hand with a worried expression.

"Will you both come?" Perce asked.

"I think so," Perce's mother said carefully. "As long as it's not *too* 'interesting'." Perce hoped it was, but didn't say anything. They pulled on the rest of their clothes, went downstairs and headed for the front door.

"Where do you think you're going?" their mother called.

"Out," Perce replied. They had the day off, after all; there were plenty of things for them to get up to in the village even while their friends were at school.

"Oh no you don't," their mother said, following them down the stairs. "If you're not at lessons, you can go and help your father." She handed Perce a pair of packed lunches. "He's re-tiling the smithy roof. You can hold the ladder. Off you go."

Perce groaned, but took the lunches, and set off to join their father at work.

*

"Now," their father said, and Perce concentrated, and the end of the soldering iron began to glow red-hot. Their father drew it swiftly and smoothly down the gap between the tiles, melting the fat tin wire he'd laid there. The metal flowed out to fill the gap in a perfect seal, cooling quickly and setting hard. Their father peered at the tiles, then nodded.

"Nice," he said. "You're a lot easier than the forge, for sure."

Perce held the ladder as their father climbed down from the smithy roof. Truth be told, they were actually enjoying helping him at work, even if it was hot and sweaty and their damp hair kept getting in their eyes. As the village roofer he mostly put up great armfuls of yellow thatch, or clay tiles on buildings like the inn and the church – but the blacksmith's forge was a special case. When the smith was working, smoke from the forge-fire and steam from the quenching bucket got everywhere. So the roof tiles were sealed with mortar and solder, so that the smoke could only go out of the chimney, rather than filling the room and the smith's house next door.

And it turned out that using a soldering iron was much easier when your child could heat things with their mind. Normally their father had to climb down the ladder, heat the iron in the blacksmith's forge, then hurry back up and melt the tin solder before it cooled down. Perce, however, was much quicker.

Their father leaned back, stretching, and looked up at the roof.

"That ought to do it," he said. "We'll get them to check it tomorrow." Perce glanced out of the smoke-yellowed window and saw that the sun was already setting. They'd been there for hours. And they were *hungry,* even after the packed lunch. Their stomach rumbled audibly. Their father chuckled.

"Magic's hard work, then?"

"Definitely," Perce said.

"Let's get back for dinner then."

They both packed up the tools and walked out into the sunset square. The breeze was cold, especially after being in the warm forge for so long.

"You're enjoying it, then?" their father asked. "The magic?"

"It's brilliant," Perce said honestly. "It's hard, but it's brilliant."

"Nothing good ever came easy," said their father sagely. "It certainly seems useful."

"I can't do much yet."

"You can do more than most," said their

father evenly. "I'd give… well, a few fingers to be able to heat things like that. And if that's just the start… well."

Perce blushed a bit.

"It's a gift," their father continued. "You can do a lot with a talent like that." He smiled. "We're proud of you, you know."

"Even Mum?"

"Especially Mum." He laughed. "It'll just take her a while to get over all the burning, is all."

Perce laughed.

"Now let's get home," their father said. "I want to see what this wizard's got up those big sleeves of his."

14

The wagon gleamed.

Perce and their parents had been invited, but half the village had turned out to see what Gideon was up to. He seemed to have been up to plenty. The blue wagon was no longer resting on its wheels – instead, four big brass legs poked out of its corners, holding the whole thing steady. A ladder led from the ground to the roof, where a railed platform now protruded from one end, behind the unfolded, enormous, majestic telescope.

It was all brass and glass, polished to a bright shine, and, fully extended, was about twice as long as a man was tall. It was currently spinning slowly around on a huge gear, Clive cranking a handle round and round while Gideon, his robes freshly laundered and his bald pate polished, examined the mechanism and occasionally poured in oil from a little can.

"That'll do," he called to Clive, who cranked the telescope around so the eyepiece was above the platform, then stopped. He leaned heavily on the railing, out of breath. Gideon squeezed his shoulder fondly.

"I'll take it from here," he said quietly, and Clive nodded gratefully, climbing down the ladder and back into the wagon. Gideon turned on his platform to look at the crowd below.

"I see we have an audience," he said, loud enough for all to hear. "You are all very welcome to observe, but I will remind you that this is a lesson for one student first and foremost." He smiled. "Though I will try to ensure that you *all* learn something tonight."

He beckoned Perce towards him, and, feeling very exposed, Perce climbed up onto the roof of the wagon. They saw Ben and Annie in the crowd, looking tired but excited. Perce waved, and both of them waved back. That made Perce feel a little better.

"What are we doing?" they asked as Gideon helped them onto the roof.

"For once," Gideon said, "not magic. Tonight, we are going to get some perspective."

He turned to the great telescope and cranked the turning-handle a few times, then adjusted some other wheels and dials. He bent to the eyepiece and checked, then grunted in satisfaction.

"Take a look at this," he said, and ushered Perce forward. There wasn't much room on the roof but they squeezed around and peered into the telescope. At first there was just darkness, but then their eye adjusted. They had expected to just see stars. But there was a big circle there instead, glowing gently and with red and orange stripes, like a stone they'd once found in the river. There were tiny white dots scattered around it.

"That's not a star," Perce said.

"It is not," Gideon agreed. "That is Jovia. That is another world."

Perce very nearly fell off the wagon.

Gideon's explanations were calm, gentle, as he cranked the telescope around and showed Perce *four* more planets. Each was a different size – a different distance away – each had its own colour, its own speckling of moons.

"And they all go round the sun," Perce said, remembering a meandering lesson from Father Tully, who came into school every so often to ramble about the gods and where they lived. His stories were always a bit vague, but Perce remembered a few of the more solid details.

"Indeed," Gideon said approvingly. "All in

a delicate cosmic harmony." He pulled a long book from his robes and showed it to Perce. On the open page there was a drawing of many large ovals, overlapping, with a large circle in the middle. Perce frowned, then understood.

"Which one is ours?"

Gideon pointed to the third oval, which had a little circle halfway around.

"There we are," he said. "Not too hot, not too cold. We would live very differently, had we been born on any of these other worlds."

"*Do* people live on them?" Perce asked.

"We do not know," said Gideon. "It is one of the many mysteries I would like to solve, if I have time."

"Can magic make you go into *space?*"

"In theory. Nobody's tried it yet." Gideon grinned. "Not *yet.*"

He turned to face the crowd.

"The point," he said loudly, so they could all hear, "of this lesson is *perspective*. How many of you have journeyed outside this county?" About half the villagers raised their hands. "Beyond the River Lud?" Several hands went down. "To the High City?" One hand stayed up; that of Father Tully.

"Without wishing to be rude," Gideon continued, "the world you know is *small*. It is the way of things. Most of us are born, live and die within the same few miles. Within the same horizon. But even if you *have* travelled this whole wide world, it is still so little." He pointed up into the sky. "We are just one of those stars. One of millions. We are so *small*.

"But we know it. And when you are so small, there is only one way you can go. We get better. We *think bigger*. We expand our minds, and we expand our world." He glanced at Perce. "Magic is one way. But it is not the only one."

The audience didn't seem *that* impressed. Most of the adults remained stony-faced.

Perce's parents looked at least half-interested. But a few of them were looking at the sky in wonder, and the children – especially Annie and Ben – were visibly amazed.

"We," Gideon said to Perce quietly, "will look at more of this later." He raised his voice. "Now, who wants to see another planet?"

Many of the villagers began to drift away, but a small queue formed immediately. Gideon rubbed his hands together.

"There's that life lesson again, Perce," he said. "They always love a show."

"Maybe you should have been an actor," Perce muttered. But Gideon just laughed.

15

By the time the church bells tolled the eleventh hour, most of the villagers had gone home. The children, who had been up and down the ladder to peer into the telescope time after time, had had to be carried sleepily away. But now it was just Gideon and Perce on the wagon, and their parents, Father Tully, and a couple of others sitting in the street below. Clive had brought out tea and folding chairs. It was cold, but Perce was full of the warmth of knowledge. And of their magic. And of one of Gideon's spare robes, which was much too big but very soft.

They were cranking the telescope

themselves now – with Gideon's help – learning to read the little etched numbers on the brass gauges and dials, and matching them to the numbers in Gideon's almanac. There were huge tables of angles and dates, all telling you exactly where each star would be found in the sky at a particular time of year. It had taken a while to get their head around it, but Perce felt like a natural now, as they tilted the telescope up to find the Dog Star high above.

"Why's it the Dog Star?" they asked, peering into the lens and finding the bright blue dot right in the centre. Gideon looked to check, and nodded approvingly.

"It is named after a legendary hound," he explained. "Did you ever hear the story of –"

In the distance, there was a *crash* like a breaking window.

Gideon froze. Perce was looking around, as were the remaining adults below, standing and frowning as they tried to figure out where the sound had come from. But Gideon had closed his eyes and was standing perfectly still, as if listening to… the silence.

"West," he said softly. "About seven hundred yards. Three… no, four people, at least."

"How…" Perce asked, but Gideon simply opened his eyes and said "Magic." But he wasn't smiling.

He called down to the adults below. "I'm going to investigate. I suggest you make for the church and be ready to ring the bells."

"It's probably nothing," offered one of the adults.

"Probably," said Gideon, "is not definitely. Stand ready. I will send word." He climbed swiftly down from the wagon, Perce following, as Father Tully led the adults away. "Perce," Gideon said, "go with them."

"I want to –"

"I will not," Gideon said sharply, "put you in danger. Go with your parents. Now."

As if to underline how serious he sounded, there was another distant *crash*. Perce scowled, but as Gideon strode off towards the noise, they followed their parents to the church.

…and then, as soon as Gideon was out of sight, they doubled back and followed him instead.

Perce was young, and small, and light on their feet. They had plenty of experience sneaking around where they weren't supposed to. The shadows were a home to them. Gideon, on the other hand, was a tall, loud old man in brightly-coloured robes – so about as conspicuous as possible.

But Perce almost lost him within thirty seconds.

Somehow, Gideon was moving silently – *really* silently. Perce saw him step on and snap a twig, but it made no sound at all. His bright blue robes looked oddly faded too, even when he passed through a pool of lanternlight. It was as though all the colour had leached out of him. When he walked in the shadows, he was almost completely invisible. *Magic?* Perce thought. But what sort of magic was this? Fire, water, air and earth couldn't make a man silent and invisible.

But it was working. Perce followed Gideon at a short distance, as quietly as they could. They were going across the edge of town to the west road that led into the woods. As they came closer to the source of the noise, Perce started to hear voices. When Gideon stopped, crouching down behind one of the last outbuildings, Perce stopped too, and strained their ears to listen.

"…breaking stuff," a man's voice was saying. "You'll wake them up."

"They're just villagers," a gruff woman replied. "Sleepy villagers."

"There's still more of them," the man snapped back. "So hold it in until we're ready. *Then* you can break whatever you like."

"And take it," said another voice gleefully.

"All that ale and wine, all that *money,* ready for the festival."

"And that wizard'll have more than we can carry," muttered someone else with glee.

"Exactly," said the first man. "But we stick to the plan. We wait for Johnson to send the signal and then we all go in *together*. So, everyone arm up, get ready, and let's take this lot for everything they've got."

There was a gentle clinking, the sound of metal on metal, padded with cloth so it wouldn't clatter loudly. The sound of weapons.

"Bandits," whispered Gideon, just loud enough for Perce to hear. "About a dozen. All armed." He looked around, straight at Perce. "I know you're there, Perce." He smiled humourlessly when Perce stepped slightly out of their shadow. "Stubborn child," he admonished. "But you can take the message for me. Get to the church and tell Tully and your parents. It's a raid. There's at least one other group of them."

"Why are they here?" Perce asked. Gideon looked slightly embarrassed.

"For your festival," he said. "And… probably for me. I am not exactly subtle when I travel."

"Are you rich?"

"Richer than them, at least." He sighed. "Maybe I should not have come back."

"What do we do?" asked Perce. The question snapped Gideon out of his guilt.

"Do you have a militia?" he asked. "A constable, even?"

"Not really." Whetstone was such a small village that they didn't bother with a proper guard, except for some nights when a shift of farmers would wander around town with pitchforks and clubs. If anyone got in trouble, all they had to do was shout, and someone at the church could sound the alarm.

"Well tell them to rouse anyone they can," Gideon said. "And to be ready to fight back, just in case."

"What about you?"

"Once you ring those bells," Gideon said, "I will keep them busy." Perce stared at him. He was a wizard, yes, and very impressive in those bright robes – but he was also an old man, *one* old man, against at least twelve armed raiders.

"I can handle myself," Gideon said. "And this is my mess, at least in part. I must clean it up. Now go, quickly!"

Perce hesitated, then ran off towards the church, as quietly as they could. They didn't hear any more breaking windows behind them, didn't hear any shouting. Hopefully they still had time. They skidded to a halt in the main square, ran up to the doors of the squat church tower and knocked, hard. A little window slid open at eye-level, and their father looked out.

"There you are!" The door opened and he gathered Perce up in a hug before they could say anything. "We were worried sick," he scolded.

"I know," Perce said, freeing themself. "Sorry. No time. Bandits." They explained everything Gideon had said. Their father went pale.

"Right," he said. "Best ring those bells."

They hurried to the back of the church, where the old priest Father Tully was lighting lamps at the bottom of the tower with Perce's mother.

"Bandits," their father snapped, and made for the bell-ropes. They all came to help him. There were two bells, and they were big, heavy things. Father Tully couldn't ring them on his own anymore. The adults all gathered round.

"Smooth pulls," instructed Tully. "All together now. *Heave.*"

The adults pulled. The bells began to ring. And from outside the church, Perce could suddenly feel heat – not on their skin, but inside their mind. A familiar heat. A fiery heat.

They ran to the window and looked east. It was the middle of the night, but there was an orange glow.

"Fire," they whispered. Then they shouted, so the adults would hear over the pealing bells. "FIRE!

16

The bells rang loud and clear.

Bandits were one thing. A fire was much, *much* worse. A group of armed men might rob them blind, or even kill somebody, but a fire – in a town of mostly wooden houses with roofs made out of dry straw – would burn down the whole of Whetstone if not stopped. Now the bells were ringing to get *everyone* out of bed, to fill the nearest bucket, and get to the flames as quickly as possible.

And that, Perce decided, meant them too.

Because Gideon had said there were *two*

groups of bandits. His group were in the west. The fire was to the east – which meant it must have been the second group. Everyone in the village would flock towards the fire to put it out… which meant the bandits wouldn't be anywhere near it. It was a distraction.

Gideon couldn't be in two places at once. The adults were busy. That left Perce.

They snuck out of the church in the confusion and headed east. There were already shouts of alarm and calls for a bucket chain ringing in the air. Perce didn't go to the fire. They knew Whetstone better than the back of their hand. The bandits *wanted* people to go to the burning house, which meant they wanted people to go *away* from somewhere else. Like the winding street that came up from the meadows and into the centre of town behind the smithy. It was open and easy to watch – unless everyone was distracted. Now, it was an open route right into the middle of Whetstone.

Perce climbed onto the thatched roof of the house behind the smithy and looked down onto the meadow road. It was empty, the door ajar – whoever lived there had run into town towards the flames. But Perce had been right. Six people in dark clothes and bits of battered armour were creeping towards town. They had a mix of battered swords and cruel-looking axes and knives. All of the blades had been blackened with soot so they didn't shine in the moonlight. They weren't here for anything good.

Just shouting for help wouldn't work, Perce thought. Nobody would hear them over the rest of the noise – and, they noticed, one of the bandits had a crossbow. Perce didn't fancy getting shot. They needed to distract the bandits and get attention some other way. They looked around for something to throw, something to break.

Then they remembered that they were literally a wizard.

Perce looked at the first bandit, took a deep breath, and reached for their inner fire.

The bandit frowned, shifted his grip on his slightly rusty sword, then yelped and dropped it on the cobbles with a clatter. One of the others swore.

"What the hell are you playing at?"

"It *burned* me," the first man said, confused. "It burned my hand."

On the roof, Perce grinned. Hot metal was hard to hold. But it had taken a lot of effort to make the sword that hot. They were already tired. But they focused, and did it again, this time to a woman further down the line, who stifled her scream but bent over her scorched hand in pain.

"Someone's doing this," said another bandit. "Someone's using magic."

The bandits clustered together, looking around. The ones Perce had disarmed drew daggers to replace their still-hot swords. Perce ducked behind the roof as far as they could. *Don't spot me,* they pleaded. They wished they could blend into the dark like Gideon. Hiding would have to do.

"Spread out," one of the bandits ordered. "They must be close. *Find them.*"

Perce had never wanted to run away as badly as they did now.

But they stayed. Because the bandits would see them if they ran. Because they were frozen in place with fear. But mostly because they were the only one who knew that the bandits were there.

It's me, Perce thought, *or nobody.*

They drew on their remaining strength, and set the nearest bandit's shirt on fire.

It took a moment for the man to notice, but then he was yelling in pain and surprise, trying to pull the shirt off but his chainmail and belts getting in the way. Two of his friends ran over to help him, but the other three kept looking around, sharp eyes peering into the gloom. *Come on,* Perce thought. *Somebody just hear this!*

The people who lived in the nearby houses were peering through their windows, a few peeking out of the doors, but when they saw the bandits they ducked back inside, scared. *They can't see me either!* Perce realised. The people didn't know that there was anyone *to* help. Perce were on their own.

They tried to heat up another sword, but it was a real strain now. Their magic was *trying* to do what Perce wanted, but it was faltering. They gritted their teeth. *Don't fail me now.* It was like they were dragging the power through thick mud. But it came, and they looked around the roof to strike again —

— and a crossbow bolt nearly took their head off, slicing through the air and clipping their ear in a bright flash of pain.

"There!" one of the bandits shouted. "It's just a kid! Up there!"

Perce darted back from another bolt, scrambling further up the roof as the bandits rushed towards them. They saw the bandit with the crossbow reloading, knew that they were the biggest danger. Perce let their magic out, and the string of the crossbow smouldered, stretched, then snapped. *No more of that!* But the bandits were already trying to climb onto the roof. Perce stamped on the first set of fingers that they saw, retreating up to the apex of the roof. Perce had disarmed the bandits but they had lots of weapons. They were bigger, meaner, and angrier than Perce. And Perce was *tired,* the magic draining them almost dry.

But they could hear shouting, the sound of people coming closer, coming to help. Whetstone knew that something was wrong. The bells had roused them, and Perce and Gideon had slowed the bandits down. Perce had done their job saving the town. Now somebody needed to save *them.*

The first bandit made it onto the roof. Perce didn't have the strength to heat his dagger.

So they apologised silently to whoever

owned this house, and set fire to the roof
instead.

17

It hadn't rained in a few days. The straw was dry as bone. Perce didn't have much magic left to give it, but they only needed a spark. The roof underneath the bandit's feet erupted into flames.

The bandit leapt back off the roof, shouting in shock and pain. Perce heard them land badly and winced. The other bandits stopped climbing, as the fire spread rapidly around the edge of the roof, given a little nudge by Perce. They were shielded by a wall of flames.

A wall of flames that was also burning up

the roof under *their* feet, of course.

There was a thick wooden beam across the top of the house and Perce scrambled up to stand on that. It would take longer to burn. They looked down at the village, and could see people starting to come towards them and their *new* fire. People in the other houses and the bandits were all yelling. Perce's plan had worked! Mostly.

"You're going to burn up there," shouted one of the bandits. "Put it out!"

"You'll just kill me," Perce shouted back. "No thanks!"

"No we won't!" the bandit replied. "A magic kid? You're worth a king's ransom! Come down and we'll let you live. Even sell you off to someone who'll treat you well." The bandit shrugged. "It's better than burning!"

"It doesn't sound like it," Perce yelled. The flames were licking higher. *Come on, somebody,* they thought. *Help!* They shouted it too, as loud as they could. But they doubted anyone would hear.

Then there was a rumble of thunder, and it started to rain.

The sky had been clear. Perce had been looking up at the bright stars. But now there were clouds, rushing in far too quickly. The rain hissed on the burning roof – not quite enough to put it out, but enough to stop the fire spreading.

It had to be magic. But it wasn't Perce.

Gideon walked into the street below. His beard had lost its point, hanging raggedly from his chin. His robes were torn in several places. But his wand was in his hand, and his eyes were burning brighter than the fire.

"Leave," he said to the bandits, his voice loud and clear. "Leave this town, now. I have already dealt with your friends. Leave, or face the consequences."

The bandits – except the one who'd fallen off the roof – gathered in front of him, their weapons drawn.

"And *there's* the wizard," said the woman who seemed like the leader. "The reason we're all here! You're the one who should run, old man." She raised her blade. "Or you can hand over your gold, and we'll be off."

"I have no gold to give you," Gideon said. "And I don't think I would do so even if I did. I will warn you again. Get out of this town, and *go*."

The bandit leader laughed.

"Looks like we'll just have to take your money off your corpse." She snapped her fingers, and pointed her sword at Gideon. *"Get him."*

The bandits charged. Gideon sighed.

"I warned you."

He twitched his wand, and spoke a word, and lightning struck.

The bolt struck the bandit leader in the

chest. For a moment she stood there, frozen –
but then she was blasted off her feet. She
knocked two of the other bandits down as she
flew. The remaining two yelled angrily, and
kept running, weapons raised.

Gideon spoke another three words. Perce
had never heard the language, but it was
somehow familiar. The ground under the
bandits' feet rumbled, then broke open. The
bandits fell ankle-deep into the hole,
stumbling. Then the ground *closed,* just as
suddenly, trapping their legs in solid earth and
stopping them dead.

The other two bandits had gotten to their
feet, leaving their leader where she lay. One of
them threw a knife at Gideon, but with a
gesture – not with his wand, but with his hand
– the wizard stopped the spinning blade in the
air, then took it. The bandit drew another knife
to throw. Gideon muttered something, and *his*
knife glowed red-hot – and he threw it back,
twice as fast. It went straight through the
bandit's knife-hand and knocked him down.

There was one bandit left standing. He looked at Gideon, looked at his wounded friends, dropped his sword and ran.

Gideon's shoulders slumped, and the storm became a drizzle. Suddenly, he was just an old man again, wet and ragged and tired. The wounded bandits moaned on the ground in front of him, but he ignored them. He turned to Perce.

"You'll have to help me," Gideon called. He raised a hand towards the fire. "I can't do it on my own." Now that he was facing them, Perce could see just how tired Gideon looked. *He just fought six bandits,* they thought. No – he'd just fought *eighteen* bandits, with the other group across town.

"You didn't teach me how," Perce shouted back, more accusingly than they'd meant to.

"Nothing like learning on the job," Gideon replied. "And you already *know.* I've seen you do it!" He flexed his fingers. "The fire was in you once. Reach for it. Pull it back!"

Perce raised shaking hands. They had pulled heat out of boiling eggs or cups of tea. They had never pulled it from an actual fire. Their hand, the one that had been burned, the one that was still slightly too pink, throbbed with remembered pain.

But it was this, they reasoned, or burn. For the fire was growing strong again.

"On three," Gideon called. "One, two —"

Perce reached for the flame, with their hands and their mind. They felt it there, hungry, devouring. It was exulting in the chance to *burn,* consuming the straw with glee.

Come back, they thought, trying to seize the heat as they had done before. *Come back to me.* But the flame refused. It wavered, when Gideon joined Perce's effort, and grew weaker… but it still burned. It was happy. It did not want to go.

I will let you burn again, Perce promised. They felt the embers of the fire within themselves, and blew on them, rousing the last of their strength. *Come back to me. Be my fire again.* Be *me.*

And, reluctantly, the flame did. Perce felt it flow into them, felt the rush of heat, of power. It was intoxicating. They dragged the fire into themselves, and with Gideon's help, it died. But Perce wanted more. They grabbed at every scrap of heat there was. The air around them grew cold, the drizzle turning to snow as it touched their shoulders. They felt something searing hot, a source of more heat and power than the sun, and reached for it – then realised what it was. It was Gideon.

"*Enough,*" Gideon said firmly. "That's enough, Perce. It's out. You can stop."

Perce wanted more. The fire within them was a greedy thing. For a moment, they wanted to ignore Gideon. *He's not using it,* part of them said. *Take it.* But the fire was out, and all the magic in the world couldn't mask the fact that they were wet and cold and *tired.*

They cut their magic off, and felt a wave of

fatigue wash over them. They stumbled, but caught themselves before they fell straight off the roof. Gideon nodded. There was something strange in his eyes.

Later, Perce would realise that it had been fear.

"Come on down," the old wizard said wearily. "There's still a lot to do."

18

Perce didn't get to bed until almost noon the next day. Gideon hadn't lied when he'd said there was a lot to do.

Of the eighteen bandits, nine were lying, burned and broken, in a locked room off the church hall. Two of the village's burliest farmers were guarding the door with pitchforks and heavy clubs. Six of the rest had managed to run away.

The other three were dead. Stories of what Gideon had done were flying around the village, each more outrageous than the last. He had summoned a daemon; he had conjured an inferno; he had turned their bodies inside-out. If Perce hadn't literally seen him call lightning from the sky, they would have scoffed at every story.

But Gideon had. And though he and Perce were at the centre of the town's recovery, everyone was keeping a respectful – or fearful – distance from them.

Seven houses had been set on fire, including the one Perce had burned. Only one had burned to the ground completely, thanks to Gideon's intervention – and nobody in the town had died, though there were a lot of burns going around, some of them serious. Perce's mother had emptied Gideon's wagon of every medicine and tincture it had, and with the help of Clive and Father Tully was patching up the whole village.

Perce and Gideon's first job had been to go around and put the rest of the fires out completely. Gideon's storm had helped, but the embers had still glowed dangerously. Perce had followed Gideon's lead – the old man was tired, but not so tired that he couldn't turn their task into a lesson.

"Pull the heat from the fire," he said, "and then just let it *out*." He was standing in front of a smouldering house, one hand pointed at it, the other facing the sky. As Perce watched, the embers and small flames began to fade and flicker. Above Gideon's other hand, the air began to shimmer with heat.

"The longer you practice magic," Gideon continued, "the more energy you will be able to hold within you. But for you, now, it cannot be too much."

"What happens if I'm too full?" Perce asked, raising their hands and copying Gideon. The heat seemed to flow *through* them, in through one hand and out through the other, and they had to fight the urge to simply drink it all in.

"Many things," said Gideon. "None of them are good, in the long term. Take in too much at once, and you *will* die."

Perce nodded. That was reason enough to listen to Gideon. But they couldn't help but think about how much power Gideon had to hold, to be able to do the things he had done.

They had felt it, earlier, when they'd nearly drunk that power in. It had been like staring into a star.

They went around two more houses before Perce dared to ask.

"The bandits," they said hesitantly. Gideon sighed. He looked very tired.

"Yes," he said. "I stopped them. I hurt them, and I made them run."

"They didn't all run," Perce said, and Gideon frowned, looking at his hands.

"I do not enjoy violence," he said. "I did not *want* to kill them. But they left me no choice."

"How did you learn… things like that?" Perce asked. "The lightning, and the knife?"

Gideon leaned back against the wall of the house, his hands still raised to draw the heat from the fire. When he spoke, his words were heavy with memory.

"When I was young," he said, "I was an apprentice, like you. I learned magic and science and all such things at my master's feet. I learned how to wield the elements, and the higher elements, and how to use them in concert. By the time I reached adulthood, I was very good at it." He smiled faintly. "If they liked me, the masters called me a prodigy. If they didn't, they called me an upstart. Either way, I was gifted."

"And then you became a wizard?"

"I had just received my staff," Gideon said. "I was not a full master yet, but I was qualified. It was traditional for young mages like me to go out into the world before they received master's robes. To travel, to learn. It is a good tradition. One day, I hope you will do the same."

The thought of going beyond Whetstone scared Perce. But it was exciting too.

"So did you do that?"

"Sort of," Gideon replied with a sigh. "I got to see the world. But not in the way I had wished."

"What happened?"

Gideon flexed his hands, and Perce felt a rush of heat as he drew the rest of the fire into himself. The embers went black.

"There was a war," said Gideon. "A vast, terrible war. It lasted years. It killed thousands." He grimaced. "And I fought in it. For it was a war of magic as well as men."

"The *Winter War?*" Perce asked. They'd learned a little bit about that in school, but only a little. But they *did* know that it had been long before Perce was born. Long before their *parents* had been born.

Just how old *was* Gideon?

"The Winter War," Gideon confirmed heavily. "It was a war of magic. A war *about* magic, in many ways. So we wizards and witches and sorcerers all took up arms, as it were. We became battlemages. We fought, and we killed, and we died." He sighed.

"I wish I had not. I wish I had not had to learn the things I did. But I did. I fought from the start of the war until its end. I learned to use my magic for violence. To destroy. And I came to loath it.

"When the war was over, I almost gave up magic entirely. I *did* give up my old life. So many of my friends just… went back to normal, when it was over. They returned to their apprenticeships, their studies, their jobs. I could not. I could not face that world."

He looked at Perce.

"I am sorry," he said. "I will not burden you with any more."

"It's alright," Perce said. "Sometimes you just need to talk." Gideon chuckled.

"You are wise beyond your years, young Perce."

He straightened, dusting his tattered robes off.

"It was the Winter War that made me into a wanderer. I built my wagon and simply set off into the world. I was looking for ways to make magic… good again. To use it to create, instead of destroy. To help people. I thought teaching you would be a good thing."

He looked down at his hands.

"And yet I find myself destroying once again. I know it was necessary. But that doesn't mean I like it."

When he looked at Perce, it was with a stare more solemn than they had ever seen.

"You have magic too," he said. "If you can burn wood, you can burn flesh. And so much more. How does that make you feel?"

Perce swallowed. Their mouth was dry.

"It scares me," they said, honestly. "I hurt the bandits because I had to. But you... you did more. If I can do that, one day? I'm scared I *will* do it." Their hand throbbed where it had been burned, all those weeks ago. "I've already hurt myself," Perce said. "What if I hurt someone else? What if it had been a house, not a chicken-coop? What if I had *meant* to burn it?"

"That," said Gideon, "is the burden of power."

Then he smiled.

"But the *point* of power," he said, "is that you do not *have* to."

19

It was not until the next day that Gideon explained what he meant.

Once the fires were put out and the injured tended to, everyone went to bed, except those on watch. Perce was asleep before they hit their pillows. They did not wake until well after noon the next day, and even then they still felt tired. To their surprise, their mother didn't complain, but simply brought them tea.

"Gideon said you needed rest," she said, perching on the edge of the bed and stroking Perce's hair. "You over-exerted yourself, he said. I can tell he was right."

Perce tried to sit up, but failed magnificently. Their mother smiled.

"Rest. You've earned it. You saved us all."

"Gideon saved us," Perce began, but their mother shook her head.

"Without you he'd not have gotten there in time. His words, not mine."

Perce lay back and frowned. *Maybe I did help more than I thought.*

"Nobody was hurt too badly," their mother continued. "Nothing was burned that can't be replaced. We're all going to be alright."

She stood up.

"So get some rest," she said, "and then come down and have something to eat. And then Gideon would like to see you at the wagon, whenever you're ready."

Perce dozed off again for another hour, then forced themself out of bed and downstairs to eat. It was easier than they'd thought. Their *mind* was tired, overwhelmed from so much magic and so much fear. But their body, apart from a few aches and pains, was full of energy. *The fire,* Perce thought, smiling quietly as they ate. *It renewed me.* All the energy of the flames was within them, just waiting to come out at their command.

If they let it. Their smile faded. *If I want to hurt someone. If I want to destroy.*

But they finished their stew, and then wandered through the village to Gideon's wagon. Their mother came with them. Everyone waved at Perce as they passed. Some people even cheered. There was, to their surprise, no fear in their eyes. Respect, yes — but not fear. It made them feel a lot better.

What they saw outside Gideon's wagon made them feel better still.

A fire had been built in the field behind the wagon — a broad, low one, the sort whose flames do not reach high but burn very hot. Clive was pouring tea from a steaming kettle.

Most of the village's children, and quite a few adults, were gathered around the fire, watching Gideon, who had a chicken leg on the end of his wand, and was explaining exactly how to cook it to perfection.

"…just until the skin starts to blacken," he was saying as Perce approached. "If you do it right that should be enough. Of course, it's much easier…"

Perce heard a familiar *sizzle,* and Gideon winked at the children as his wand glowed hot.

"…if you've got a few tricks up your sleeve." He popped the chicken onto a plate that was already piled high with steaming barbeque. "Taste and see."

He passed the plate of barbeque round. As everyone tucked in, Gideon walked over to Perce and their mother, wiping his wand clean on his robes. He nodded at Perce's mother, who nodded back – not warmly, Perce saw, but respectfully. It was a start.

"I'm going to get something to eat," said

Perce's mother, and she went over to the fire and the other villagers.

"You look well-rested," said Gideon to Perce. Perce nodded.

"It's weird," they said. "I was so tired, but so full of energy." Gideon nodded sagely.

"Magic is a fickle thing. It fills you up and wears you out all at once." He looked like he'd gotten some sleep too, though there were still dark rings under his eyes. He had changed into a clean and undamaged robe too, and combed his beard.

"Come," Gideon said. "Sit with me."

The ladder was still out from the night before, and there was just enough room on the raised platform for both Perce and Gideon to sit up on the wagon's roof, above the milling villagers below. Gideon dangled his legs through the railing like a child. They looked down on the village. The burned buildings were still smoking slightly. But the sun was shining, and there was the sound of laughter and birdsong on the wind, as the villagers started once again to prepare for the spring festival.

"Last night," said Gideon, "we destroyed. We hurt, with our magic. It was necessary. We could have done far worse. But it is still not a pleasant way to use our power."

Perce wondered what worse things there were than killing. But Gideon was still talking.

"But there are *other ways,*" Gideon said. "That is the beauty and the curse of our gift. We can do *anything,* if we have the skill and the passion to learn how." He gestured to the people below, clustered around his fire. "We can douse fires as well as start them. We can look into the heavens and see other worlds. We can cook *fantastic* food." Perce laughed. Gideon grinned. "You see? Just because we have the potential to do terrible things does not mean that we must. And even if we must, they need not be without good reason."

Perce thought about it.

"You could say that for anyone," they said reasonably. "We *all* choose what we do, don't we? With the talents we have? We all choose to do good things or bad things."

"You are not wrong," Gideon admitted. "All of us have potential, whether we know it or not." He looked down at the children below again. "Especially you young people. You have the power to do anything you set your minds to." He winked at Perce. "We magicians just have a head-start."

"I can do anything," Perce murmured. And as the wind blew and the sun shone, for the first time, they really believed it.

"You can," Gideon echoed. "You really can, Perce. Once you are trained, the world is yours. You could become an artificer, a stargazer, a healer. You could advise kings or build cities. You could become a warrior, too. But only if you *want* to."

"Or a travelling chef," said Perce. Gideon laughed aloud.

"Well, I am getting old," he said. "Maybe one day I'll give you the wagon and build myself a restaurant." Perce laughed too.

They sat and watched the sky for a few moments.

"Really anything?" Perce asked.

"Once you're trained," Gideon said. "Which will take a while yet, so don't get too many ideas."

"I thought I was doing well?" Perce said, frowning.

"You are. At what you've learned. There's an awful lot more where that came from." Gideon clicked his fingers, and a leaf on the wind suddenly veered towards him and began to spin around his upraised hand.

"I'll be on lightning in no time," Perce promised.

"I think," Gideon said, "that you actually will." He looked Perce in the eye. "We have not known one another long. This may not mean much. But I'm proud of you."

It meant plenty.

"Now," said Gideon, "let's head back down and practice something that's not fire, shall we?" Perce groaned. "We've both got energy to spare," Gideon admonished, making the leaf spin on the tip of his finger before letting it go. "Let's use it."

"Show me the leaf thing," Perce demanded.

"Why not?" Gideon said, standing and stretching. "It's a new day. It's time for new things."

They climbed down from the wagon, walked into the field, and began to learn the secrets of the wind.

AFTERWORD

Well, there you go. A book for children. That was a lot of fun to write.

I've been writing science fiction and fantasy for about 8 years now, but I've always written for adults (or at least not specifically for children). But working at the wonderful Toy Project means I've been spending a lot of time *with* children, and talking about the sorts of stories they enjoy reading.

So I thought 'how hard can it be?' The answer is *quite hard,* especially when you've spent 8 years writing for grown-ups! But I think it's turned out alright.

My thanks to Jane, Jess, Emma and Artie, for proofreading this book together and showing me all the bits I'd done wrong. I hope I fixed all of them.

Perce, Gideon and Clive will return. I've got plenty more planned for them – if nothing else, Gideon still has a barbeque technique to perfect.

Until then, thanks for reading. I hope you enjoyed it.

Printed in Great Britain
by Amazon